Let's Explore Math

A Journey in Four Parts

Part 1: Exploring Multiplication
Part 2: Exploring Division
Part 3: Exploring Fractions
Part 4: Exploring Money

STORY & VISUALS BY **ALICE ASPINALL**

ILLUSTRATIONS BY **ALEXANDRIA MASSE**

Enjoy the four parts in this book as individual math stories. Then, have fun making connections between them!

Check the back of the book for exploration questions and helpful resources.

Let's Explore Math: A Journey in Four Parts
by Alice Aspinall

Published by EduMatch®
PO Box 150324, Alexandria, VA 22315
www.edumatch.org

ISBN-13: 978-1-953852-16-8

Thank you to my best friend and life partner
for always supporting me.

Thank you to my children for
encouraging my storytelling with
remarkable enthusiasm.

Part 1: Exploring Multiplication

Math Vocabulary

altogether – including everything

cylinder – a 3-dimensional figure with circles on both ends

estimate – roughly calculate

multiples – the answers when multiplying a number by other numbers; ex: the multiples of 10 are 10, 20, 30, 40, 50, etc.

Reading Vocabulary

announces – says to a group of people

confident, confidently – without doubt

fades – disappears

glee – happiness

impressive – awesome or excellent

overwhelmed – feeling heavy with emotions

It's free-play time in class and Amy and Johnathan are playing with the foam blocks. "Let's build a tower!" shouts Amy.

Johnathan is excited for this idea. He responds, "Great idea! We can make it a **cylinder** and then we can hide inside. Let's figure out how many blocks we need for the bottom row." Johnathan and Amy start placing foam blocks side by side until they form a circle on the ground. "Fourteen blocks for the first row," Johnathan **announces**.

"I'll get more blocks for the next row," shouts Amy, walking away.

Johnathan stops her and says, "Wait, Amy! Let's **estimate** how many blocks we will need **altogether** so we can just get them all at once."

"How are we supposed to know how many blocks we are going to need for the entire tower?" Amy asks curiously.

"It looks to me like we could make it 12 rows tall and we would have an **impressive** tower! So, we just need to figure out how many blocks we need to make 12 rows with 14 blocks in each row," says Johnathan **confidently**.

The smile on Amy's face **fades** immediately. She bows her head down and says, "But that is a multiplication problem. I can't do 12 x 14. Those numbers are way too big."

Johnathan pauses to think and then says, "Let's start by thinking of easier numbers first. I know that 12 x 10 is 120 by skip counting by tens. This means we will need at least 120 blocks. Amy still looks unsure.

"We can figure this out together, Amy, but first I think we need to clear our minds so we can relax. Let's try the breathing our teacher, Mrs. Garcia, tells us to do when we are feeling **overwhelmed**," Johnathan says calmly.

Johnathan and Amy ground their feet firmly on the floor, close their eyes and take three deep breaths together. They open their eyes and smile at each other.

Johnathan starts the problem again, "If 12 x 14 is too big for us, let's break it down into numbers that are easier for us to manage. For me, sometimes **multiples** of 10 are easy to do. We can break up 14 as 10 + 4. This means we can try 12 x 10 and 12 x 4 and put them together. Remember, from our **estimate**, that 12 x 10 is 120."

$$12 \times 14$$
$$= 12 \times (10 + 4)$$
$$= (12 \times 10) + (12 \times 4)$$
$$= 120 + (12 \times 4)$$

"Well, I don't know what 12 x 4 is, but I do know that 12 x 2 is 24 because I remember when my mom bought two dozen eggs at the store once," recalls Amy.

$$= 120 + (12 \times 4)$$
$$= 120 + 12 \times (2 + 2)$$
$$= 120 + (12 \times 2) + (12 \times 2)$$
$$= 120 + 24 + 24$$

"If 12 x 2 is 24, then 12 x 4 is two groups of 24. 20 + 20 = 40 and 4 + 4 = 8. Forty-eight! 12 x 4 is 48!" Johnathan says with **glee**. Amy smiles back and begins to feel more **confident** than she did before.

$$= 120 + 24 + 24$$
$$\qquad\quad 20 + 4 \quad\;\; 20 + 4$$
$$= 120 + 20 + 20 + 4 + 4$$
$$= 120 + 40 + 8$$
$$= 120 + 48$$

Amy stops for a moment, then thinks out loud,
"We have 120 and 48. If we add those
together, we get 168!" She jumps
up and down with excitement.

Johnathan joins in the celebration, "Yes, we did it! Those
numbers were definitely not too big for our teamwork. Now
let's start counting blocks and get this tower built!"

You have read
one fourth
or
one quarter

$$\frac{1}{4}$$

of this book!

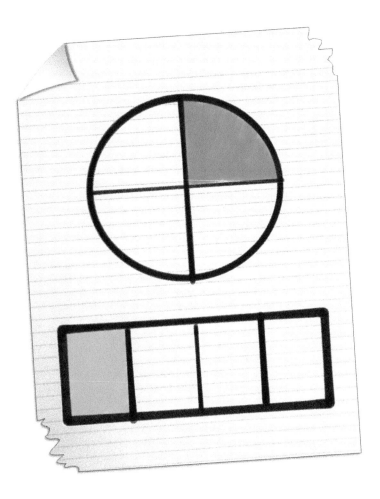

Part 2: Exploring Division

Math Vocabulary

brainstorm – come up with ideas

equal – to be the same

multiple – the answer when multiplying a number by another number; ex: the multiples of 8 are 8, 16, 24, 32, 40, etc.

Reading Vocabulary

chuckles – laughs quietly

confirmation – to see if something is true

satisfied – happy

unison – at the same time

Amy and Miles are playing outside at recess. Luciana walks up through the crowds of students and asks them if they would like to join in to play a new card game she made up last night. "It uses two decks of cards and lots of people can play at once. Come play with us!" Luciana says.

They join the group happily and Luciana begins explaining the set up for the game, "Each player needs the same number of cards to start. There are eight of us here."

Miles asks, "How many cards are in one deck?"

"Fifty-two," Luciana replies and continues, "Two groups of 52 makes 104 cards in total. We have to divide those into 8 **equal** groups."

Amy's eyes start to look worried. Luciana notices her friend doesn't look happy. "What's wrong?" she asks Amy.

Amy tells the group, "You all do this math in your heads so quickly and I can't keep up! Now you're about to do a big division problem. I don't even know how to start figuring out 104 ÷ 8."

Luciana does not want her friend to feel this way and replies, "I don't know the answer to that problem either, Amy, but I know we can do this together. But before we start, remember what Mrs. Garcia would say – we need to loosen up our bodies to allow our minds to work. Let's try ten jumping jacks!"

All the children stand up and count out ten jumping jacks in **unison**, then they sit back down and start to **brainstorm**.

Miles offers some help and says, "I know that 80 is a **multiple** of 8 because 8 x 10 = 80. This means that 80 ÷ 8 = 10. Does that help?"

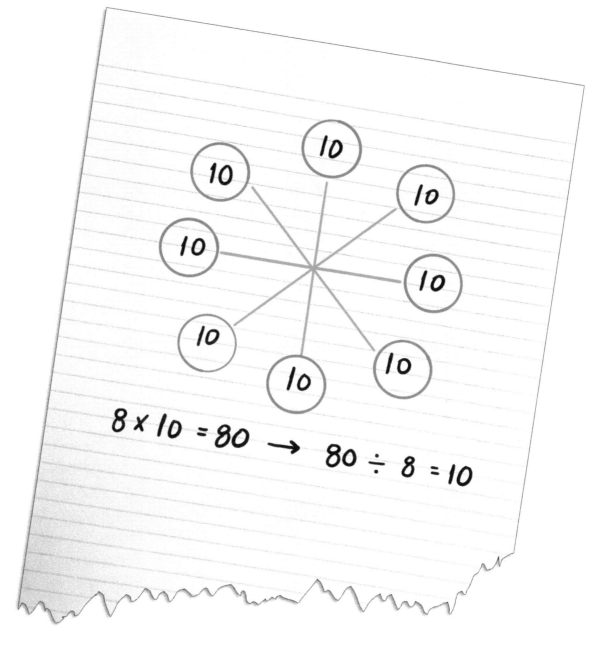

"We have 104 cards, not 80," replies Amy sadly.

Luciana thinks for a minute and raises a finger to show she has an idea, "You're right, Amy, we do have 104 cards, but we can divide the 80 by 8 first and then worry about the remaining cards. If we give everyone 10 cards, that is a total of 80. How many would we have left in the deck?"

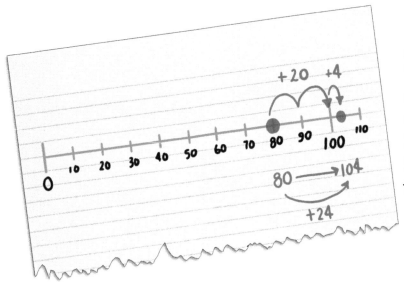

Amy thinks aloud, "From 80 to 100 is 20, and then we have 4 more. This makes 24 left over cards. So, I guess we need to do 24 ÷ 8 next."

"Yes!" exclaims Luciana, "We have broken down 104 ÷ 8 into (80 ÷ 8) + (24 ÷ 8)."

Miles shouts, "I know 8 x 3 = 24, so 24 ÷ 8 must equal 3!"

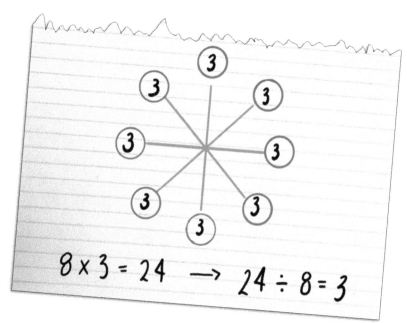

Everyone is **satisfied** with this answer. Amy continues, "Everyone first got 10 cards and now they need 3 more. This means each of us should have a total of 13 cards each. Is that right?" She turns to Luciana for **confirmation**.

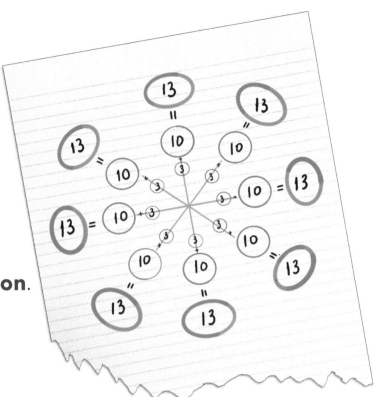

"That is exactly right. That was hard work, but we figured it out! Now let's play this game," **chuckles** Luciana.

You have read
two fourths
or
two quarters
or
one half

$$\frac{2}{4} = \frac{1}{2}$$

of this book!

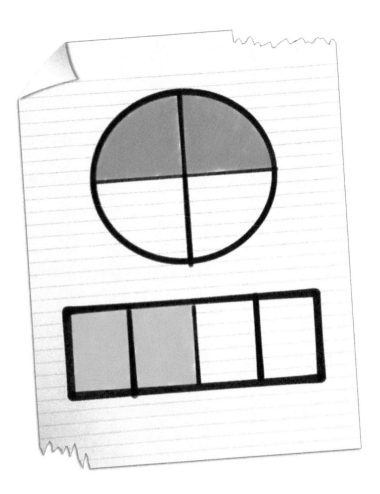

Part 3: Exploring Fractions

Math Vocabulary

fractions – parts of a whole

quarters – pieces created by cutting something into four equal parts

whole – one complete object containing all parts

Reading Vocabulary

announces – says to a group of people

chimes in – enters the conversation

eagerly – with excitement

impressed – showing approval of something

overwhelmed – feeling heavy with emotions

pita bread – round, flat bread

Amy is having a birthday party with all of her friends at her house. The kids are playing Hide-and-Seek while her mom is busy getting ingredients ready because Amy and her friends are going to make mini pizzas together.

Amy's mom calls the children into the kitchen and says, "Okay everyone, we are going to make mini pizzas using **pita bread**. We will cut each pizza into four pieces leaving us with **quarters** to eat. Earlier, I asked each of you how many quarters of a pizza you would like to have for dinner and I made a list. This is what I gathered: two friends want 3 quarters each, two friends want 4 quarters each, two friends want 5 quarters, and one friend wants 2 quarters."

Immediately, Amy's excitement turns into sadness in front of all her friends and she sighs, "Oh no. This sounds like **fractions** to me."

"You guessed it!" says Amy's mom, "But I think we can figure this out together. What does everyone think?"

Johnathan **chimes in** happily, "Of course we can figure this out! But if you're feeling **overwhelmed**, Mrs. Garcia would tell us we need a break. Who's in for a quick dance party first?"

Amy's mom turns on some music and all the kids dance around the kitchen for five minutes. She turns off the music and everyone gathers around the table once again.

"Can you show us your list again, Mom?" asks Amy. She writes out her thinking on the bottom of the paper.

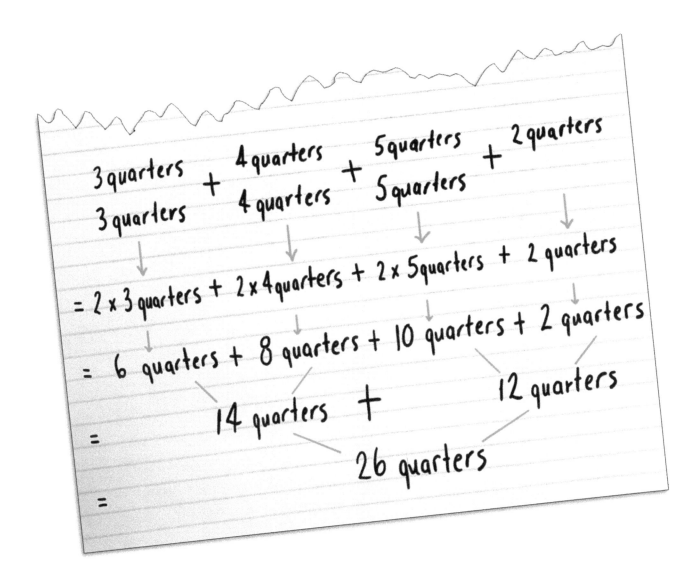

Amy **announces eagerly**, "I know that we need 26 **quarters** of pizza!"

Amy's mom is very **impressed**, "Wow! That's some good thinking there, Amy. Can anyone help us write 26 **quarters** in a different way?"

Miles has been waiting patiently for his turn and finally says, "Yes, we should figure out how many **whole** pizzas we need so that it's easier to make them."

"Good idea, Miles! I can count by fours:
4, 8, 12, 16, 20, 24. That is 6 groups of 4 to get 24 quarters. This means we need 6 whole pizzas," Luciana uses her fingers to count the six groups. She is quite proud of herself.

$$\frac{4}{4} + \frac{4}{4} + \frac{4}{4} + \frac{4}{4} + \frac{4}{4} + \frac{4}{4} = \frac{24}{4}$$

$$1 + 1 + 1 + 1 + 1 + 1 = 6 \text{ whole pizzas}$$

Miles looks confused now and replies, "But we need 26 **quarters**, not 24."

"Right, Miles, we will have 2 quarters left," replies Amy. She stops to think for a minute. Everyone is silent. Then, she stands up a little taller and says proudly, "Two quarters is the same as one half. We will need 6 **whole** pizzas plus one half of a pizza."

$$\frac{2}{4} = \frac{1}{2} \text{ pizza}$$

$$6 \text{ whole pizzas} + \frac{1}{2} \text{ pizza} = 6\frac{1}{2} \text{ pizzas}$$

Johnathan gives his friends a smile and says, "**Fractions** are no problem for us! Now, who's hungry?"

You have read
three fourths
or
three quarters

$$\frac{3}{4}$$

of this book!

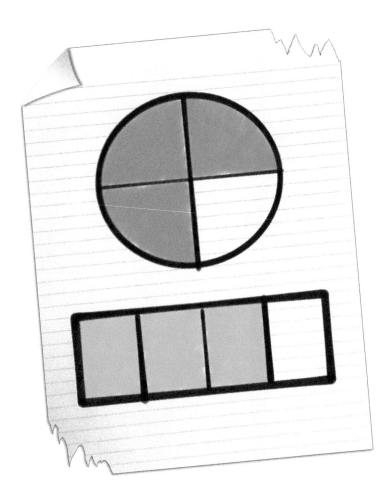

Part 4: Exploring Money

Math Vocabulary

brainstorming – coming up with ideas

concludes – states the final answer

quarters – coins worth 25 cents each ($0.25)

sorted – organized in groups with matching characteristics

summarizes – gives the final answer quickly

whole – one complete object containing all parts

Reading Vocabulary

admits – tells the truth

alphabetical order – putting things in order following the same order as the letters in the alphabet

browse – look through

complicated – having many different parts combined together

grimaces – makes an unhappy face

headspace – mindset or how someone is feeling mentally

interrupt – to stop someone who is speaking

intimidated – scared

pensive – a look that shows someone is thinking hard

slumps – falls heavily

Amy is visiting Johnathan's home after school. She walks into his house and sees that he has books laid out all over his living room floor. This is very unlike Johnathan because he is usually so tidy.

She asks him, "What is going on here? You always keep your things so organized."

Johnathan **grimaces** and **admits**, "I normally have my books on the shelves in **alphabetical order**, but I'm trying to earn some money to buy a new video game. I've decided to sell some of my older books."

Amy lights up and eyes the books on the floor saying, "I would love to buy some books for my collection! How much is each book?"

"My parents think I should ask $2.00 for hardcover books and $1.25 for paperback books. Take a look through and see which ones you want," Johnathan replies. He exits the room to grab some water and leaves Amy to **browse** through the books.

When Johnathan returns with two glasses of water, Amy shows him the books she has picked out. She has them **sorted** into two piles and says, "I have chosen 3 hardcovers and 5 paperbacks. I have $15.00 in my school bag. Is that enough money? Sometimes I get confused when dealing with money." Amy **slumps** down on a chair and looks away.

"Wait a second, Amy. You can figure this out. You don't need to be **intimidated** by money problems. But right now, you are not in the right **headspace**. We need to focus our thoughts before we can tackle something difficult – that's what Mrs. Garcia always says. Come over to the table with me; I have paper and pencils out and I know you like to draw," Johnathan says as he walks to the kitchen table and Amy follows behind him.

Johnathan and Amy sit together and doodle page after page of **complicated** swirls and lines making beautiful patterns and designs for ten minutes. They giggle together and share their designs. When they pause, Johnathan says, "Let's get back to that money problem."

Amy turns over one of the pages she's drawing on and begins **brainstorming**. She thinks aloud, "I chose 3 hardcover books that cost $2.00 each. I know that is 3 x $2.00 which makes $6.00 for the hardcover books." She writes this on the paper.

"Good. Now let's deal with the paperback books. You chose 5 of them and they each cost $1.25," says Johnathan as he points to Amy's paper. Amy writes down this information.

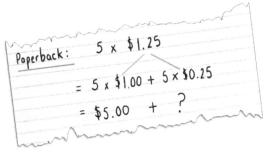

Hardcover: 3 x $2.00 = $6.00

"I think I can break this down. I know that 5 books at $1.00 each would be $5.00. That leaves 5 **quarters** to add up," Amy says. Then she draws five $0.25 coins on her paper.

Paperback: 5 x $1.25
= 5 x $1.00 + 5 x $0.25
= $5.00 + ?

Johnathan points at her drawing and says, "Let's count by 25s together."

As he points to each coin, he and Amy count together slowly, "25, 50, 75... $1.00."

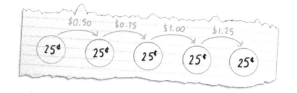

$0.50 $0.75 $1.00 $1.25

25¢ 25¢ 25¢ 25¢ 25¢

"Wait – four quarters make one **whole** dollar. That makes sense!" Amy says.

Then, Johnathan points at the last quarter on the drawing and they both shout, "$1.25!"

Amy picks up her pencil and continues to write while telling Johnathan, "So, we have $5.00 plus $1.25, which makes $6.25 for the paperback books."

= $5.00 + $1.25
= $6.25

"Awesome work! Let's put it all together. We had $6.00 for the hardcovers and $6.25 for the paperbacks. If we add those together, we get a total of $12.25 for all the books you want to buy," Johnathan **concludes**. Then he takes a pencil and writes on Amy's paper, "You have $15.00. Can you find the change I owe you?"

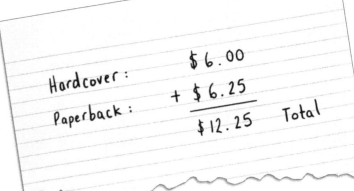

Amy looks very **pensive** and takes a moment before she speaks, "Mrs. Garcia told us that a good way to make change is to start at the amount you are paying and count up to the amount you have."

"I remember that! We need to start at $12.25 and count up to $15.00. We can go from $12.25 to $13.00 by adding $0.75, right?" Johnathan asks.

"Yes, I think that works. Then we need to count from $13.00 to $15.00. I can do that – it's $2.00!" Amy is getting excited because she knows they are close to solving the problem.

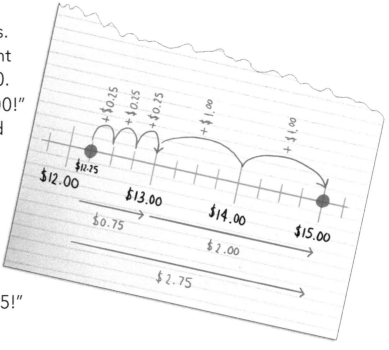

Johnathan can't help but **interrupt**, "$0.75 + $2.00 is $2.75!" He is excited, too.

Amy sits back in her chair and **summarizes** their work, "I owe you $12.25 for the books and you owe me $2.75 in change from my $15.00."

"We did it, Amy! We solved this money problem. I think we can solve any problem if we talk it out together. Now let's celebrate with a snack!" Johnathan and Amy give each other a high-five and skip over to the fridge together.

You have read
four fourths
or
four quarters

$$\frac{4}{4}$$

of this book

or

1

one whole
book!

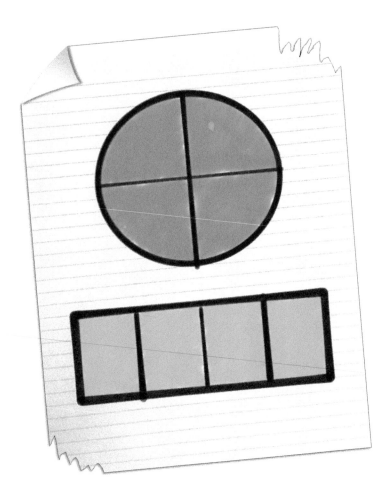

For Educators and Families

Discussion Questions

Before Reading

1. Pose the problem from each part of the book to children before they read the story to see how they would go about solving it themselves.

    Part 1: You want to build a cylindrical tower out of foam blocks. You need to decide how to make 12 rows with 14 blocks in each row. How many blocks will you need to build the tower?

    Part 2: You are going to play a card game with your friends. You need to distribute 2 decks of cards among 8 friends. How many cards will each kid receive?

    Part 3: You are having a party and you're making mini pizzas with your friends. This is the list of pizza that everyone wants: two friends want 3 quarters each, two friends want 4 quarters each, two friends want 5 quarters, and one friend wants 2 quarters. How many total pizzas do you and your friends need to make?

    Part 4: Your friend is selling books to raise money for a new toy. You are going to purchase 3 hardcover books for $2.00 each and 5 paperback books for $1.25 each. How much will the books cost altogether? How much change does your friend owe you if you pay them with $15.00?

2. Ask: What do you do when you get overwhelmed or frustrated when working on a difficult problem? What helps you calm down so you can concentrate?

During Reading

1. You may decide to pause throughout each story to have children continue working through the problems.
2. Ask: What might you do differently than Amy and her friends to solve this problem?

After Reading

1. Ask: What strategies do Amy's friends suggest as brain breaks when Amy gets frustrated?
2. Brainstorm a list of other ideas that you could use when your brain needs a break.
3. Ask: Amy and her friends use a lot of mental math strategies when solving math problems. When is it useful to use mental math instead of pencil and paper strategies?
4. Discuss a time when you used math when playing with your friends.

For Educators and Families

Extension Questions

Part 1: Exploring Multiplication

1. How would you evaluate 12 x 14?
2. How many different ways can you show that 12 x 14 = 168?
3. Could you use the same strategies to find 24 x 14? Why or why not?
4. How would you get the answer to 24 x 140?

Part 2: Exploring Division

1. How would you find 104 ÷ 8?
2. How many different ways can you show that 104 ÷ 8 = 13?
3. What would happen if Luciana only had 7 friends playing her card game? Would there be some cards left over? How many?
4. How many cards would each person get if Luciana only used one deck of cards and only 4 people were playing the game? How does this compare to the original problem?

Part 3: Exploring Fractions

1. How can you show 26 quarters using fraction notation?
2. How would you simplify 26 quarters?
3. How many different ways can you show 26 quarters?
4. How would the number of whole pizzas change if Amy and her friends only needed 21 quarters?

Part 4: Exploring Money

1. How would you find the total cost to buy 3 hardcover books and 5 paperback books?
2. What other ways could you use to find the change Amy needs back from $15.00?
3. Would Amy have enough money to buy 4 hardcover books and 6 paperback books from Johnathan?
4. How would the total cost and the change be different if Johnathan charges $1.75 for each hardcover book instead of $2.00?

For Educators and Families

Other Resources

Free online resources that foster a math mindset and a love of math:

1. Adding Parents to the Equation: facebook.com/groups/addingparents
2. Bedtime Math: bedtimemath.org
3. Counting with Kids: countingwithkids.com
4. Illustrative Mathematics: illustrativemathematics.org
5. Math at Home: mathathome.org
6. Math Before Bed: mathbeforebed.com
7. Math is Visual: mathisvisual.com
8. Math Recess: mathrecessbook.com
9. Table Talk Math: tabletalkmath.com
10. Talking Math with Your Kids: talkingmathwithkids.com
11. Which One Doesn't Belong?: wodb.ca
12. YouCubed: youcubed.org

Praise for LET'S EXPLORE MATH

Perfect read aloud! This book puts children front and center, illustrating the strategies used to persevere through difficult math concepts. Showing that it is conceivable to find joy in math. A book that is sure to make a difference at home and in the classroom.
- Rosalba Serrano, Math Consultant and Founder of *Zenned Math*

Alice Aspinall does it again! This book is a fun way to explore different math concepts and address that some students face anxiety. She introduces brain breaks, math and reading vocabulary, and gives resources at the end that will help any parent or educator in helping students develop and enjoy a math mindset. I enjoyed the realistic stories and math concept introductions. I know students will enjoy this and put healthy practices in place.
- Melody McAllister, Educator and Author of *I'm Sorry Story*

As a father of four kids, I am so excited about this book. Alice has a masterful way of making math make sense. She takes the abstract and makes it tangible. This is a book that will get a lot of use in my house.
- Dr. Dave Schmittou, Professor of Education and Author

I only wish I had a book like this when I was learning all of those important math skills! I love the mind/body connection to calming those anxious math feelings before tackling big problems. This is an important lesson for all students and adults to practice when doing math. The visual break downs of each problem as Amy and her friends are working out the problems is so powerful and really helpful for the reader. This is a book that keeps on giving with the math lessons, visuals, calming strategies, discussion questions and additional math resources. I can't wait until I have this in my hands for my children at home and in school!
- Valerie Sousa, Kindergarten Teacher & Author

Motivating students to like math is so important because it can be so challenging at times. The positive approach to this topic, not without struggle, helps us all (kids included) to see the potential they have to think about math in more than one way. I love the theme of teamwork as it is a necessary element for us all to know and practice. Thanks for pushing us to love math and be open to trying things differently.
- Dene Gainey, Educator - ELA/Drama, Author of *Journey to the Y in You*

Alice Aspinall, B.Math(Hon), B.Ed, is a Portuguese-Canadian secondary mathematics educator in Ontario, Canada. She loves spending time with her husband and two children reading books, playing math games, and exploring the outdoors.

Alice is a strong advocate of the growth mindset. She is continually looking for ways to build young people's confidence in math and to make math fun, challenging, and satisfying. Her innovative lessons and her dedication in the classroom have made a positive impact on her students' attitudes toward math.

Alice is also a champion for females in STEM by encouraging girls to pursue science and mathematics both in high school and in post-secondary education. Alice believes everyone can learn math and she is on a mission to prove it.

Ontario based illustrator, Alexandria Masse, creates simple, yet emotive and colourful images for children's books. She completed her first book at the end of high school. Some of her books include: *Everyone Can Learn Math, Hallway Connections, Think Like a Coder, Gracie, and Finding Lost Smiles*. She believes that stories can come to life through her illustrations. Alexandria currently resides in Halifax with her pet rabbits, where she is studying fashion and textiles on a full scholarship at NSCAD University.

EduMatch Publishing

CPSIA information can be obtained
at www.ICGtesting.com
Printed in the USA
LVHW071619150921
697894LV00015B/1934